FROM THE ENCHANTED TALES OF
HANS ANDERSEN

The LITTLE MERMAID

First published in Great Britain by Beehive Books, an imprint of
Orbis Publishing Limited, London, 1986.

Text and illustrations
© Mushroom Writers' and Artists' Workshop Limited, 1986.

This edition © Orbis Publishing Limited, 1986.
The Enchanted Tales of Grimm and Andersen are produced by Mushroom
Writers' and Artists' Workshop Limited, 9 Newburgh Street,
London, W1V 1LH.

Printed in Belgium by Proost
Origination by Newsele SRL (UK)
Typeset by Chambers Wallace of Drury Lane in Monophoto Baskerville

ISBN 0 85613 945 9

FROM THE ENCHANTED TALES OF
HANS ANDERSEN

The LITTLE MERMAID

BEEHIVE BOOKS · LONDON

Your mother, the Sea Queen, has made a rule that none of the merprinces and merprincesses is allowed to visit the overworld until he or she is fifteen years old.

You've always wanted to be a human but it's ages until your fifteenth birthday. You know that Poseidon, God of the sea, gives every merchild three wishes as a birth gift, so you could ask him to make you human. But your mother has warned you to save your wishes for times when you really need them.

Your grandmother told you a legend that a merchild can become human if a human prince becomes his or her best friend. You decide to find a prince.

Start looking on page 1.

The quads, your sisters Thetis, Aruthusa, Scylla and Eurydice, are fifteen today. They are allowed to go to the surface for the first time. They spend hours preening themselves, plaiting pearls and rare pink seaweed in their hair, hanging dozens of coral chains round their necks and clipping eight oysters to their tails, to show that they are princesses.

You're jealous. Why shouldn't you go to the surface with them, just because you're the youngest? You decide to go too.

Follow Thetis. Go to page 7.
Or follow Scylla. Go to page 26.
Or follow Eurydice. Go to page 18.
Or follow Aruthusa. Go to page 36.

Suddenly someone surfaces beside you. You recognize the eskimermaid who saved you from the ice. Then another face appears – a blubbery, whiskered face.

'My friend the walrus will help,' says the eskimermaid. 'Selsius, will you rescue that young man?'

The walrus plunges into the turbulent sea and gently takes the prince's coat in his mouth. Then he tows him away from the wreckage.

'Find the nearest land,' calls the eskimermaid, diving again.

If you have decided to make this prince your best friend, try to become human. Ask the sea-witch for help. Go to page 23.
Or, if you want to talk to the prince and see if you like him, follow the walrus. He will drop the prince in shallow waters near land. Go to page 17.

The prince decides that you must have been shipwrecked. 'You'd better come with us,' he says, 'unless you're afraid of sailing on rough seas.'

You laugh to yourself, and shake your head.

The prince's sister explains, 'We're going to fetch my brother's bride, a princess who saved him when *he* was shipwrecked.'

On board ship, everyone is amazed at how nimble and quick-footed you are.

'I'm going to give you to my bride,' says the prince. 'You'll make the perfect companion.'

That evening you collect the princess. Later that night your sisters surface by the ship. They throw you a knife.

' "Companion"! Servant, he means,' says Scylla. 'You won't stay human unless the prince is your best friend. We bought this knife from the sea-witch. Use it to cut off his bride's hair. He'll soon fall out of love with her, and you'll be his only friend.'

If you want to use the knife, go to page 22.
Or throw it back into the sea. Go to page 30.

The bulbous tips of the polyp fronds sway on the current, searching for prey. You wrap your arms tightly round yourself and tuck in your fins. Then, with a flick of your tail, you dart forward.

But you've forgotten the strings of pearls trailing from your wrists. They brush against a polyp. Instantly its tentacles wrap round you and hug you stickily.

You can't escape – unless you start again – from page 1.

The sailors swing you over a big glass tank, then open the net. You drop into salt water. A man comes to stare at you, and you poke out your tongue at him. He laughs and calls, 'Look at this, Captain; you might almost think it could understand.'

The captain looks at you. 'It's the perfect exhibit for your menagerie, Colonel,' he says. 'You'll have to train it to do some tricks – jump through hoops and things.'

You listen to the sailors talk, and learn that the ship is full of strange and rare creatures collected by the Colonel. He is on his way to a command show at the royal palace.

The ship docks at a busy port and the animals are unloaded. Something huge and fierce is led down the gangplank. It tries to stampede and the whole ship rocks. Your tank is almost overturned. Water slops out.

If you want to use your chance to dive overboard, go to page 9.
Or, if you've already been home to page 9, go to page 24.
Or, if you want to stay on the ship, go to page 8.

You're not afraid of the storm, and you ride the big waves easily. Suddenly a dazzling flash lights up the sky. A lightning bolt strikes the ship's mast. Cr-r-a-a-sh! It falls, smashing through the deck and bashing a hole in the hull. The sea pours in, breaking up the ship to matchsticks. Sailors are jumping overboard and swimming for dear life. The captain steps on deck, and you hear him shout, 'Prince! Prince! Your Highness must jump!'

A young man comes out of the cabin and follows the captain to the rail. They both jump, but a wave throws a piece of ship's timber in the young man's path. He is knocked out, and goes under.

If you want to rescue the young man, go to page 10.
Or, if Phorcys is with you, go to page 11.

Impatient Thetis streams up to the surface the second she has clipped the last oyster to her tail. You follow her trail of bubbles. Your first sight of the upper world is horribly disappointing. You nearly gasp, 'But there's nothing here!' but bite your tongue; you can't help wondering what all the fuss is about.

You are about to turn for home when you hear Thetis pulling herself out of the water. Your eyes soon get used to the dark, and you see that she is lying on a sandbank. Then you notice lights on the horizon. As dawn breaks, you realize that it's a ship. You've never seen a whole one before, only wrecks.

If you would like to see this one more closely, go to page 13.
Or, if you want to see what your other sisters are doing, find Scylla.
Go to page 26.
Or follow Aruthusa. Go to page 36.
Or follow Eurydice. Go to page 18.

The Colonel loads his menagerie on to a cart and drives to the royal palace. He sets up his show in the courtyard, and labels your tank, '*The world's one and only merchild*' (the liar!).

The royal family come to see the exhibits. The king is delighted with everything, especially the mandragora and the hydra. He asks how many people the Gorgon has turned to stone. The queen wants to buy the unicorn. But the prince lingers by your tank.

'I'm sure its not happy in that tank,' he says. 'I'm going to make the Colonel sell it to me.'

Bang your head on the glass to show the prince that you understand. He will buy you. Go to page 14.
Or, if you don't want to be 'bought', shake your head. The prince will have you emptied back into the sea and you can go home to page 24.

Your mother is waiting for you. She tells
you off for going to the surface. Then she
laughs and says, 'I know it's hard being the
youngest, and it seems like ages till you're
fifteen. I can see we'll get no peace until
you go up, so swallow this magic seaweed.
Now you can breathe air for as long as you
like, not just an hour or two.'

You can't believe your luck. But you're not
so pleased when she adds, 'But you must
promise to come straight back. And dress
properly for once. If you're going into
public, you're to look like one of the royal
house, not a sea urchin.'

She wants you to wear strings of pearls on
your wrists and oysters clipped to your tail.
If you are willing to do anything to get to
the surface, agree. Wait until you see a
ship going over and follow it. Go to page 35.
Or, if you hate wearing uncomfortable things,
refuse, and go to page 13.

You see Eurydice and Scylla sitting on a rock, combing their hair and singing. You call to them to help you save the prince.

'Mermaids don't rescue humans,' says Eurydice. 'They let them drown.'

The sailors are climbing into a raft and steering it towards the captain, who is swimming strongly. They seem to have forgotten the drowning prince. The waves toss him to the surface again and roll him on to a piece of the ship's mast. But how long will he stay afloat?

If you are wearing your valuable pearls and oysters, you can use them to bribe your sisters. They will drag the prince to the shallows near a beach. Go to page 17.

Or, if you have given the oysters and pearls away, call on Poseidon for help. He will calm the water and leave the prince by a safe beach. Go to page 17.

Or, if you have used up your wishes, you'll have to start again. Go to page 1.

Or, if you have met an Eskimermaid, go to page 2.

Phorcys streaks through the foaming water and dives. He comes up with the prince on his back, and carries him to you. Together, you take him to a small island in calm water.

When the prince wakes, you tell him about the shipwreck. Instead of thanking you for rescuing him, he says, 'Well how am I going to get home from here?'

'I don't know,' you say. 'This island is a long way from the mainland. Far too far for Phorcys to carry you.'

'Well I can't stay here,' says the prince crossly, 'with nothing but fish for company. I shall go mad.'

Help the prince to build a raft and take turns in pushing him until you meet a ship to take him home. Then go to page 24.
Or make him stay on the island. Go to page 27.

The prince sits up and groans,
'Where am I? Where is my ship?'
You explain about the shipwreck.

'Did you rescue me?' he asks. 'You saved my life! But how did you survive the storm? How can you stay afloat in such rough seas?'

'Easily!' you tell him. 'I can swim in any sea.' You lift the end of your tail proudly.

The prince recoils in horror. 'Ugh!' he gasps. 'You're a fish!' He wrinkles his nose in disgust. 'You mean you *touched* me?' he demands. 'How revolting! Are you slimy like a fish?'

You dive down deep, to cool your burning cheeks in the sea.
If you want to forget this nasty, insulting prince, go home. Go to page 24.
Or, if you can forgive him, stay out of sight just under the surface, and keep watch. Go to page 33.

The ship is hung with strong nets and lines. You decide it must be a fishing boat. Then you spot something floating in the water. You swim closer, and see that it's a funny sort of transparent lobster pot. Inside is a seahorse, swimming round and round in panic-stricken circles and bashing its little head against the glass walls. You hurry to let it out.

Suddenly a net drops down over you. You try to dive under it, but your tail is caught between the ropes. The more you leap and wriggle, the tighter the net is pulled. Then there is a jerk, the ropes grow taut, and you are lifted out of the sea. As you swing over the ship you hear a voice say, 'That was a good bait all right. It caught us a merbrat.'

Ask Poseidon to rescue you. Go to page 25.
Or, if you have used up your wishes, try to escape by yourself. Go to page 5.

The prince has you taken to the royal swimming pool. 'I'm sure it will be happier in there than in a tank,' he says.

'Of course, dear,' says the queen. 'But where will we swim? And who's going to feed it and clean it out? You should think of these things before you bring home these exotic pets . . .'

'Pet!?' you yell, thrashing the water with your tail. 'I'm nobody's pet. I'm a free merchild!'

'Your new pet's making a noise,' says the queen. 'Oh! It splashed my new gown. Look! It's snarling and showing its teeth! I hope it's not dangerous. Don't go too near the edge, dear.'

They don't understand you! And they don't want you to be a friend, just a pet!

If you have a wish left, ask Poseidon to send you home, and start the adventure again, on page 1.
Or, if you have no wishes left, you'll have to stay where you are, forever!

The prince rows on. Suddenly foam appears, the water begins to bubble and boil and spray leaps high into the air, as Poseidon rises from the sea.

'Come back!' he calls. 'Come back to the sea with me! If you will dive now, I will break the sea-witch's spell.'

The prince cowers in terror, shaking like a jellyfish. 'Aaarrgh!' he gibbers. 'It's a monster! It's going to eat me! Make it go away!' Suddenly he finds a gun in the bottom of the boat. He aims it at Poseidon. Of course a paltry human bullet couldn't hurt Poseidon, but it shows you what a coward the prince is.

Abandon him and follow Poseidon. Go to page 32.
Or resign yourself to staying with the cowardly prince and being a human slave forever.

The potion burns your throat and makes your head spin. Suddenly a hundred knives seem to stab into your tail. You cry out. The sea-witch's voice comes from far away. 'Your tail is dissolving into two stumps called legs. They will carry you, but every step will feel as if you are walking on razors! And if you ever go into salt water again, you will turn into sea foam!'

You open your eyes, and see, the prince! You are on the beach below his palace and the prince and three children, who look like his brother and sisters, are bending over you.

If you have met the children before, when you were all swimming, go to page 31.
Or, if you haven't met the children before, go to page 3.

You haul the prince to the shore and push him on to the beach. It slopes too steeply for you to be able to pull yourself up beside him, so you watch his pale face anxiously. Is he breathing? You're not sure how much sea water humans can swallow before they drown.

If you are very worried about the prince, ask Poseidon to make him breathe again. Go to page 28.
Or, if you think that the prince is still breathing, wait for him to wake up. Go to page 33.

You reach the surface just after Eurydice, and find yourself at the mouth of a river. Eurydice swims upstream and you follow her, past rolling green countryside. You've never seen anything so lovely.

You pass a small lagoon. It's full of human children, tumbling and rolling and splashing each other like dolphins. You didn't know humans could swim. It isn't fair. They can live in the water – why can't you live on land?

One of the children sees you and shouts, 'Do you want to play? We're having a competition to see who can pick up the most shells from the bottom.'

You win of course. They think you're a fantastic swimmer. They see your tail, but they're not at all afraid of you, unlike human grown-ups. Suddenly you realize that you've forgotten Eurydice. She's nowhere to be seen. Look for her at home. Go to page 9.

Or find Scylla. Go to page 26.

Or follow Aruthusa. Go to page 36.

Dangling from the polyp trees are fish, seaweed, shells, bits of wrecked ships – and the skeleton of a poor mermaid. You close your eyes and hug your arms close to your sides. Then you zip forward, fast.

Phew! You are relieved to find yourself at the black mouth of a deep cavern. A shrill voice shrieks, 'Come in, child! I know what you've come for!'

You tipfin inside, shivering. There is the sea-witch, even uglier and more terrifying than you imagined.

'I will make you human,' she says. 'But it will cost you dear. You can have legs in return for – your tongue!'

If you don't want to lose your tongue, and you haven't used three wishes yet, call on Father Poseidon for help. Go to page 21.

Or, if you have used up all your wishes, let the sea-witch cut out your tongue. Go to page 16.

You leap into the sea, hoping that you can pull the prince back to the boat before you become sea foam. It's hard to swim with two stiff legs instead of a strong, supple tail, but you manage to grab him by the scruff of the neck. He's conscious, in fact he's smiling! 'It's all right,' he says. 'You can let go. I can swim. Look!' and he holds up his powerful tail.

Suddenly you realize that your clumsy doggy paddle has become an effortless glide. Your tail is back! And you don't feel as though you are standing on knives any more.

'Let me explain,' says the prince. 'I was a merprince until the evil sea-witch cast a spell on me. Until someone was willing to sacrifice themself for me, I was stuck in a human shape. You have saved me!'

You have defeated the sea-witch and won. The merprince gives you half his kingdom as a reward, and Poseidon grants you three more wishes. Your first wish could be to start the adventure again . . .

You look into the sea and you call on Father Poseidon for help. His face appears in the water. 'I will not give you legs yet,' he says. 'But if you have two wishes left, I will send you to the surface. You will be able to live there. If you don't like humans as much as you expect, you can use the second wish to come home.'

If you have two or three wishes left, let Poseidon send you to the prince's palace. Go to page 14.
Or, if you only have one left, or you don't want to see the prince again while you've still got a tail, agree to let the sea-witch have your tongue in return for making you human. Drink her potion on page 16.

You sneak into the princess's cabin and quietly cut off
her hair. 'Good!' you think. 'You look like a shorn sheep. Now the prince
won't marry you, and he'll have time for me.'

　　But when the prince sees her, he doesn't refuse to marry her, or send
her away. But he is furious. He grabs you by the shoulders and shakes
you, demanding, 'Did you do this?'

　　You nod.

　　'You little monster!' he shouts. 'You ungrateful beast!' and he hurls
you overboard.

Go to page 29.

The sea-witch's cave is at the bottom of a powerful whirlpool. Bravely you plunge in. You are whirled round and round, and sucked down and down. At last, sick, breathless and dizzy, you are spat out at the bottom. But there's worse to come! The sea-witch's cave is protected by an avenue of polyp trees. They grab anything that touches them, and hold it fast – forever.

You have to pass through the avenue to reach the sea-witch. If you are wearing strings of pearls, go to page 4.
Or, if you have given away your pearls, go to page 19.

You try to forget about finding a prince. You sit in the
palace garden, but the marble statue of a human boy
reminds you. Your sisters try to cheer you up with games of dolphin
polo. Thetis even offers to share the treasure chest she took from a
sunken pirate ship, but it's no good.

'I want to be human!' you tell them. 'I'm bored with the sea. I
want to run and ride a horse and climb trees. I want legs!'

'You'd hate being human,' Thetis tells you. 'They're clumsy and
slow and weak. They can't even breathe under water; and any
minnow swims better than they do.'

If you still want to be human, and you have met the prince, ask the
sea-witch to help. Go to page 23.
Or, if you haven't met a prince yet, try to find one. A ship is passing
overhead. Follow it, and surface on page 35.

'Great Father Poseidon,' you beg. 'Help!'

Poseidon hears you. In his cave, far below the ocean bed, he flicks his little finger. The water splashes. The splash becomes a current. The current becomes a tide. The tide becomes a crest. The crest becomes a tidal wave and rears over the ship. Then it breaks, crashing down with a deafening roar. Poseidon's angry voice commands, 'Never trap my sea creatures again!' Then he whispers, 'Remember – only three wishes.'

You are thrown out of the tank back into the sea. If you want to visit the surface again, and you haven't followed your sisters yet, follow Scylla. Go to page 26.
Or, if you haven't followed Eurydice, follow her on page 18.
Or, if you haven't eaten any magic seaweed yet, go home to your mother. Go to page 9.

You follow Scylla a long way over the sea bed before she begins to climb towards the surface. Your pet dolphin, Phorcys, follows you, despite your whispered command to go home. You're almost exhausted by the time you reach the surface, but anything Scylla can do, you want to do better. You can see her tail flipping nervously in the water, though her head and shoulders must be in the air. She is rolling in the choppy sea, clutching her ornaments. As you surface behind her, you see why. The sea is full of darting, plunging silver bodies. She has come up in a shoal of dolphins. They tumble and roll, calling Phorcys to come and play. Of course he dashes off to join them, so Scylla spots you. She's furious. 'You saucy sprat!' she yells. 'What are you doing here? How dare you follow me? Go home before I tell Mother – and don't come back until you're fifteen.'

Do as she says. Go to page 9.
Or see if your other sisters are friendlier. If you haven't followed Eurydice, go to page 18.
Or, if you haven't followed Aruthusa, go to page 36.

The prince pines for other humans: for his horses and carriages, hawks and hounds, musicians and jesters. After three days he goes into a sulk. He won't speak to you, though you and Phorcys have swum until you dropped, to find him fresh water and delicious seafood. Phorcys is bored and goes off by himself.

That afternoon, Phorcys comes swimming back, pushing something with his nose. It's a sailor's hat.

'Where did you get that?' asks the prince. 'Is a ship nearby?' Phorcys chatters excitedly, pointing to the east.

'You must carry me there at once!' orders the prince.

If you feel sorry for the prince, let Phorcys carry him away. Then you can go home. Go to page 24.
Or, if you've had enough of the prince's sulks and bossiness, tell Phorcys to leave him where he is. Find a better prince. Start the adventure again, on page 1.

'Father Poseidon,' you call. 'Please revive the prince.' Immediately a fresh wind blows in from the sea. A soft sea spray rains gently on the prince's face. He stirs.

While you wait for the prince to wake, you idly pick up a sea shell and hold it to your ear. At first you hear only the sea, then Poseidon's voice whispers, 'Don't forget, merchild, you have only three wishes. And don't forget, humans bring trouble. Have nothing to do with them.'

If you want to talk to the prince, wait until he wakes. Go to page 12.
Or, if you want to become human, and you have a wish left, ask Poseidon. Go to page 21.
Or, if you have used up all your wishes, ask the sea-witch to make you human. Go to page 23.

The instant you land in the sea you are turned into foam. The tide will dash you against the beach, drag you back into the sea, and hurl you forward again forever, unless you have one of Poseidon's wishes left.

If you have, you can start the adventure again, from page 1.

You decide that you don't want to hurt the prince's bride. You throw the knife into the sea. Next day the prince says, 'I'm going to take a break before my wedding. Come fishing with me.'

He takes you out far from the ship. While he is busy rowing, your sisters appear behind him.

'Quickly!' they whisper. 'He will make you no better than a slave. You'll hate being a human servant – it's nothing but cleaning and scrubbing and dancing attendance on her. And she'll soon be a bad-tempered hag. Leave him to us! We know how to deal with him!'

Let your sisters do as they ask. Go to page 34.
Or tell them that you won't leave the prince. Go to page 15.

The children remember you.

'Aren't you that great swimmer who picked up the most shells?' asks the youngest.

You try to answer him, but of course you can't speak.

'What's up?' asks the prince. 'Lost your tongue?'

You nod your head sadly.

'Who are you?' he continues. 'Where did you come from?'

'We know,' say the children, and they tell their brother about meeting you and learning about the merpeople.

'And you're not afraid of them?' he asks.

'Of course not,' they say. 'We're friends.'

'Then so am I,' decides the prince.

So you move into the palace and become of the human royal family. You live happily ever after, but you miss the swimming!

You leap overboard. Poseidon points his trident at you. A lightning bolt strikes you, sizzling over your skin. Your legs glue together. Fins sprout on your shoulders and sides. Webs grow between your fingers and toes. You feel your tongue stretch.

Then the lightning is sucked back into the trident. You fall into the sea, a merchild again.

'I hope you'll stay out of trouble in future,' says Poseidon. 'And be content with life underwater.'

But you're not sure. Perhaps, one day, you'll want to have another adventure . . .

Suddenly a striped beach ball lands by the prince's ear. A girl comes running after the ball, through the trees.

'Idiot,' you mutter. 'You might have broken his nose.'

The girl sees the prince and lets out an ear-splitting shriek.

'Stop being so wet,' you yell. 'Fetch help.'

'Fetch it yourself,' she says sulkily. 'Princesses like me don't fetch things.'

'I can't,' you tell her. And you lift your tail to show why.

The girl screams again, 'A sea monster! Mummy!' Dropping her ball, she runs away.

'Oh terrific,' you groan. 'So that's how humans rescue each other. The prince could die before she'd do any good.'

But some people come to see what frightened the girl. They find the prince and carry him away.

If you want to see the prince again, ask the sea witch to make you human. Go to page 23.

Or go home. Go to page 24.

Aruthusa, Eurydice, Scylla and Thetis begin to sing. They have the best voices of all the mermaids (and even a tone-deaf mermaid sings better than any human). Their sea-song sounds like the tide ebbing and flowing. They sing of the water drawing all things back into the sea: drawing back the pebbles from the beach, drawing back the sand, drawing the prince. He stands up, and steps up to the prow of the boat. The sisters sing louder, luring the prince to them. He steps overboard – and plunges into the sea! He is so entranced, he doesn't even try to swim.

If you can't bear to see the prince drown, go to page 20.
Or forget him and start the adventure again. Look for a nicer prince this time. Go to page 1.

When you reach the surface, the ship is almost on the horizon. A storm is brewing. The sails stand out against the purple clouds, and you can see the royal crest of a prince.

The wind whips up the sea, and waves toss the ship high, then drop away, letting it fall back into the churning water. You watch the sailors scurry about, hauling on ropes, unfurling canvas and battening down hatches.

The sails' canvas snaps and cracks in the wind. Suddenly a tremendous gust fills the mainsail – and tears it from top to bottom. The ship spins in a circle over the angry sea. The sailors can't escape the storm. People are thrown overboard.

Suddenly there is a deafening crash. Thunder!
If you want to help the sailors, try to stop the storm. Go to page 2.
Or watch the storm tear the ship apart. Go to page 6.

Aruthusa finishes decking herself out and announces, 'Before I go up to the surface, I'm going to visit Aunt Undine. Want to come with me?'

You agree to keep her company on the long swim to Undine's home on the other side of the sea bed.

Your aunt is delighted to see you and gives you an enormous tea. Then she gives you both presents. Yours is a flute made of whale bones. Aruthusa's is a coat of whaleskin, lined with squid.

After tea, Aruthusa says it's time for her to go. You and Aunt Undine see her off. As she spirals towards the surface, your aunt tells you to hurry home. But as soon as she goes inside, you follow Aruthusa.

You find yourself in a strange frozen world. Everywhere you look is ice. Now you understand Aruthusa's present. It's far too cold to hang around. You turn to dive again, but you can't. The sea has frozen around you!

Suddenly something pokes through the ice and begins to saw. When it has cut a circle, a round lid of ice is pushed up, and you see a friendly face underneath. It's an eskimermaid. She throws you a coat like Aruthusa's. 'Quickly,' she says. 'Dive, before the sea freezes again.'

Go home to warm up. Go to page 9.
Or, if you haven't followed Scylla before, go to page 26.
Or, if you haven't followed Eurydice before, go to page 18.